KU-615-139

FIRST FAIRY TALES

The Frog Prince

For Natalie – *MM*
For Branwen – *PN*

Series reading consultant: Prue Goodwin,
Reading and Language Information Centre,
University of Reading

ORCHARD BOOKS
338 Euston Road, London NW1 3BH
Orchard Books Australia
Level 17/207 Kent Street, Sydney, NSW 2000

This text was first published in Great Britain in the form
of a gift collection called *First Fairy Tales*,
illustrated by Selina Young, in 1994

First published in Great Britain in hardback in 2005
First paperback publication in 2006
This edition published in 2007 for Index Books Limited

Text © Margaret Mayo 1994
Illustrations © Philip Norman 2005

The rights of Margaret Mayo to be identified as the author and
Philip Norman to be identified as the illustrator have been
asserted by them in accordance with the Copyright, Designs and Patents Act, 1988.

A CIP catalogue record for this book is available from the British Library

ISBN 978 1 84362 457 8

1 3 5 7 9 10 8 6 4 2

Printed in China

Orchard Books is a division of Hachette Children's Books
www.orchardbooks.co.uk

⭐ FIRST FAIRY TALES ⭐
The Frog Prince

Margaret Mayo ⭐ Philip Norman

ORCHARD BOOKS

There was once a little princess who had seven sisters. But they were much older than her, so every day she had to play in the palace gardens by herself.

One day, she was playing with her favourite sparkling, golden ball, and it fell *splash!* into the lily pond. The princess was upset and began to cry.

Then she heard a croaky voice say, "I will find your ball. But you must give me something in return!"

She looked around and saw a
frog, sitting on a waterlily leaf.
"Frog," she said, "if you find my
ball, I'll give you my bracelet, my
necklace…anything!"

"I don't want a bracelet or a necklace," said the frog. "I want you to promise to be my friend and let me eat from your plate and sleep on your soft bed."

The princess didn't like frogs. She didn't like their bulgy eyes and their cold, damp skin. But she thought, "He's only a silly frog. I won't ever see him again." So she said, "I promise."

The frog dived into the pond.
A few minutes later, he climbed
out and dropped the golden ball
by the princess's feet.

The princess picked it up.
"Thank you," she said.

And she turned round and ran
off! "Wait!" called the frog. "I
can't run fast. I can only jump."

But the princess ran even faster.

That evening, the king, the
queen, the seven older sisters and
the little princess were eating their
supper, when they heard a strange
noise. *Ker-plump! Ker-plump!*
Ker-plump! Something was
coming up the marble stairs.

Then, a croaky voice called out,
"Little princess! Open the door
and let me in!"

The king stopped eating,

the queen stopped eating,

the seven older sisters stopped
eating.

They all looked at the little
princess. She jumped up, ran to
the door and opened it. And there
was THE FROG!

As soon as she saw him, she
banged the door shut.

"Who was that knocking at the door?" asked her father, the king.

"It was a frog," she said.

"And what does Mr Croaky Water-splasher want?" he asked.

Then she told him all about
her golden ball and the promise
she had made.

"My little princess," said her
father, "you must always keep
a promise. Now open the door
and let him in."

She opened the door slowly,
and the frog came jumping
into the room.

When he reached the table,
he said, "Please lift me up."

"Ugh!" said the princess. She
didn't want to touch the frog.

"Remember your promise," said
her father.

So the princess lifted the frog,
with one finger and one thumb,
and dropped him on the table.

Then the frog began to eat the
food on her plate.

"Ugh!" she said. "I'm not
going to eat from the same plate
as a frog!"

When the frog had finished
eating, he said, "Please carry me
up to your bed."

"No, I won't!" she said.

"Remember your promise,"
said her father.

So the princess lifted the frog,
with one finger and one thumb,
and carried him up to her bedroom.
Then she dropped him on the floor.

"Remember your promise," said
the frog. "You must let me sleep
on your bed."

So the princess lifted the frog,
with one finger and one thumb,
and dropped him on the bed,
right at the bottom.

"Please," said the frog. "I would
like to sleep on your pillow."

"No!" she answered. "I didn't promise that. Stay at the bottom of the bed." Then she climbed into bed and fell asleep.

When she woke the next
morning, the first thing she saw
was **THE FROG**. He was sitting
on her pillow, staring at her with
his bulgy eyes.

"Ugh!" she said and grabbed hold of him and threw him off the bed.

Wham! The frog hit the wall, fell to the floor and lay there.

The little princess was upset. She climbed out of bed and picked him up. "Frog, please don't die," she said. "I didn't mean to hurt you."

Then she kissed him…and the
frog was gone and there was a…
A HANDSOME PRINCE!

"Thank you, little princess!' he said. "You have set me free from an evil spell. One day, when I was riding through a forest, a wicked witch changed me into a frog.

"Only a kiss from a princess could make me a prince again!"

Well, then the little princess and the frog prince really did become good friends. And when she grew older, they married and lived happily ever after!

FIRST FAIRY TALES
by Margaret Mayo
Illustrated by Philip Norman

Enjoy a little more magic with these other First Fairy Tales:

❑ Cinderella	1 84121 150 8	£3.99
❑ Hansel and Gretel	1 84121 148 6	£3.99
❑ Jack and the Beanstalk	1 84121 146 X	£3.99
❑ Sleeping Beauty	1 84121 144 3	£3.99
❑ Rumpelstiltskin	1 84121 152 4	£3.99
❑ Snow White	1 84121 154 0	£3.99
❑ The Frog Prince	1 84362 457 5	£3.99
❑ Puss in Boots	1 84362 454 0	£3.99

Animal Crackers

by Rose Impey
Illustrated by Shoo Rayner

Have you read any Animal Crackers?

❑ A Birthday for Bluebell	1 84121 228 8	£3.99
❑ Hot Dog Harris	1 84121 232 6	£3.99
❑ Tiny Tim	1 84121 240 7	£3.99

and many other titles.

First Fairy Tales and Colour Crackers are available from all good bookshops,
or can be ordered direct from the publisher:
Orchard Books, PO BOX 29, Douglas IM99 1BQ
Credit card orders please telephone 01624 836000
or fax 01624 837033
or e-mail: bookshop@enterprise.net for details.

To order please quote title, author and ISBN
and your full name and address.
Cheques and postal orders should be
made payable to 'Bookpost plc'.
Postage and packing is FREE within the UK
(overseas customers should add £1.00 per book).

Prices and availability are subject to change.